CHESTER'S WAY

by Kevin Henkes

Greenwillow Books • New York

Watercolors and a black pen line were
used for the full-color art.
The text type is ITC Galliard.

Copyright © 1988 by Kevin Henkes
All rights reserved. No part of this book
may be reproduced or utilized in any form
or by any means, electronic or mechanical,
including photocopying, recording or by
any information storage and retrieval
system, without permission in writing
from the Publisher, Greenwillow Books,
a division of William Morrow & Company, Inc.,
1350 Avenue of the Americas, New York, NY 10019.
Reprinted by permission of Greenwillow Books,
a division of William Morrow & Company, Inc.
Printed in China
First Edition 15 14 13 12 11 10

Library of Congress Cataloging-in-Publication Data

Henkes, Kevin.   Chester's way.
Summary: Chester and Wilson share the
same exact way of doing things, until Lilly
moves into the neighborhood and shows them
that new ways can be just as good.
[1. Friendship—Fiction] I. Title.
PZ7.H389Ch   1988   [E]   87-14882
ISBN 0-688-07607-6
ISBN 0-688-07608-4 (lib. bdg.)

• For Ginny •

Hello, my name is Chester.
I like croquet and peanut butter
and making my bed.

CHESTER had his own way of doing things....

He always cut his sandwiches diagonally.

He always got out of bed on the same side.

And he never left the house without double-knotting his shoes.

Chester always had the same thing for breakfast—toast with jam and peanut butter.

And he always carried a miniature first-aid kit in his back pocket. Just in case.

"You definitely have a mind of your own," said Chester's mother. "That's one way to put it," said Chester's father.

Chester's best friend Wilson was exactly the same way. That's why they were best friends.

Chester wouldn't play baseball unless Wilson played, and they never swung at the first pitch or slid headfirst.

Wilson wouldn't ride his bike unless Chester wanted to, and they always used hand signals.

If Chester was hungry, Wilson was too, but they rarely ate between meals.

"Some days I can't tell those two apart," said Wilson's mother. "Me either," said Wilson's father.

ADVANCED CROQUET TIPS

Chester and Wilson, Wilson and Chester. That's the way it was.

They loved to go on picnics. Once, when Wilson accidently swallowed a watermelon seed and cried because he was afraid that a watermelon plant would grow inside him, Chester swallowed one, too.

"Don't worry," said Chester. "Now, if you grow a watermelon plant, I'll grow one, too."

Chester duplicated his Christmas list every year and gave a copy to Wilson, because they always wanted the same things anyway.

For Halloween, they always dressed as things that went together—salt and pepper shakers, two mittens on a string, ham and eggs.

"They really are two peas in a pod," said Chester's mother.

"Looks like it," said Chester's father.

In spring, Chester and Wilson shared the same umbrella.

In winter, they never threw snowballs at each other.

In fall, they raked leaves together.

And in summer, they reminded each other
to wear sunscreen, so they wouldn't burn.

Chester and Wilson, Wilson and Chester.
That's the way it was.

And then Lilly moved into the neighborhood.

LILLY had <u>her</u> own way of doing things....

She wore band-aids all over her
arms and legs, to look brave.

I MA YLLIL

She talked backwards to herself
sometimes, so no one would
know what she was saying.

And she never left the house
without one of her
nifty disguises.

Lilly waved at all the cars that passed by, even if she didn't know who was in them.

And she always carried a loaded squirt gun in her back pocket. Just in case.

"She definitely has a mind of her own," said Chester.
"That's one way to put it," said Wilson.

When Lilly asked Chester and Wilson to play, they
said they were busy.

When she called them up on the phone, they disguised
their voices and said they weren't home.

If Lilly was walking on one side of the street, Chester
and Wilson crossed to the other and hid.

"She's something else," said Chester.
"Looks like it," said Wilson.

One day, while Chester and Wilson were practicing
their hand signals, some older boys rode by, popping
wheelies. They circled Chester and Wilson and yelled
personal remarks.

Chester and Wilson didn't know what to do. Just when they were about to give up hope, a fierce-looking cat with horrible fangs jumped out of the bushes and frightened the older boys away.

"Are you who I think you are?" Chester asked the cat.
"Of course," the cat replied.

"Thank you, Lilly," said Chester.
"You're welcome, Chester," said Lilly.
"Thank you, Lilly," said Wilson.
"You're welcome, Wilson," said Lilly.
"I'm glad you were wearing a disguise," said Chester.
"And I'm glad you had your squirt gun," said Wilson.
"I always do," said Lilly. "Just in case."

Afterward, Chester invited
Lilly over for lunch.
"You have a Muscle Mouse
cup?!" said Lilly.
"Of course," said Chester.
"I do, too!" said Lilly.
"Same here," said Wilson.

Chester and Wilson cut their
sandwiches diagonally. Lilly asked
Chester's mother if she had cookie
cutters, and she made stars and
flowers and bells.
"That's neat!" said Chester.
"Wow!" said Wilson.

That night, Lilly invited Chester and Wilson to sleep over.

"You have a night light?!" said Chester.

"Of course," said Lilly.

"I do, too!" said Chester.

"Same here," said Wilson.

Chester and Wilson wanted toast with jam and peanut butter for breakfast the next morning.

"Boring," said Lilly. "Try this instead."

"This is good!" said Chester.

"Wow!" said Wilson.

After that, when Lilly asked
Chester and Wilson to play,
they said yes.

When she called them up on
the phone, they had pleasant
conversations.

And if Lilly was walking on one
side of the street, Chester and
Wilson waved and ran to catch
up with her.

Chester and Wilson taught Lilly hand signals. And she taught them how to pop wheelies.

Lilly taught Chester and Wilson how to talk backwards. And they taught her how to double-knot her shoes.

"Some days I can't tell those three apart," said
   Lilly's mother.
"Me either," said Lilly's father.

Chester and Wilson and Lilly, Lilly and Wilson
and Chester. That's the way it was.

For Halloween, they dressed as The Three Blind Mice.

For Christmas, Lilly gave Chester and Wilson nifty disguises. And they gave her a box of multi-colored shoelaces—extra long for double-knotting.

They loved to go on picnics. When Chester and Wilson told Lilly about how they had each swallowed a watermelon seed once, Lilly swallowed <u>three</u> of them. "I'll grow a watermelon plant for each of us," she said.

In spring, Chester and Wilson and Lilly shared the same umbrella.

In winter, they never threw snowballs at each other.

In fall, they raked leaves together.

And in summer, they reminded each other to wear sunscreen, so they wouldn't burn.

Chester and Wilson and Lilly,
Lilly and Wilson and Chester.
That's the way it was....

And then Victor moved into the neighborhood...